RIVER OF SORROWS

DENNIS PHILLIPS

PAGE PUBLISHING
Conneaut Lake, PA

First originally published by Page Publishing 2022

ISBN 979-8-88654-258-5 (pbk)
ISBN 979-8-88654-261-5 (digital)

Printed in the United States of America

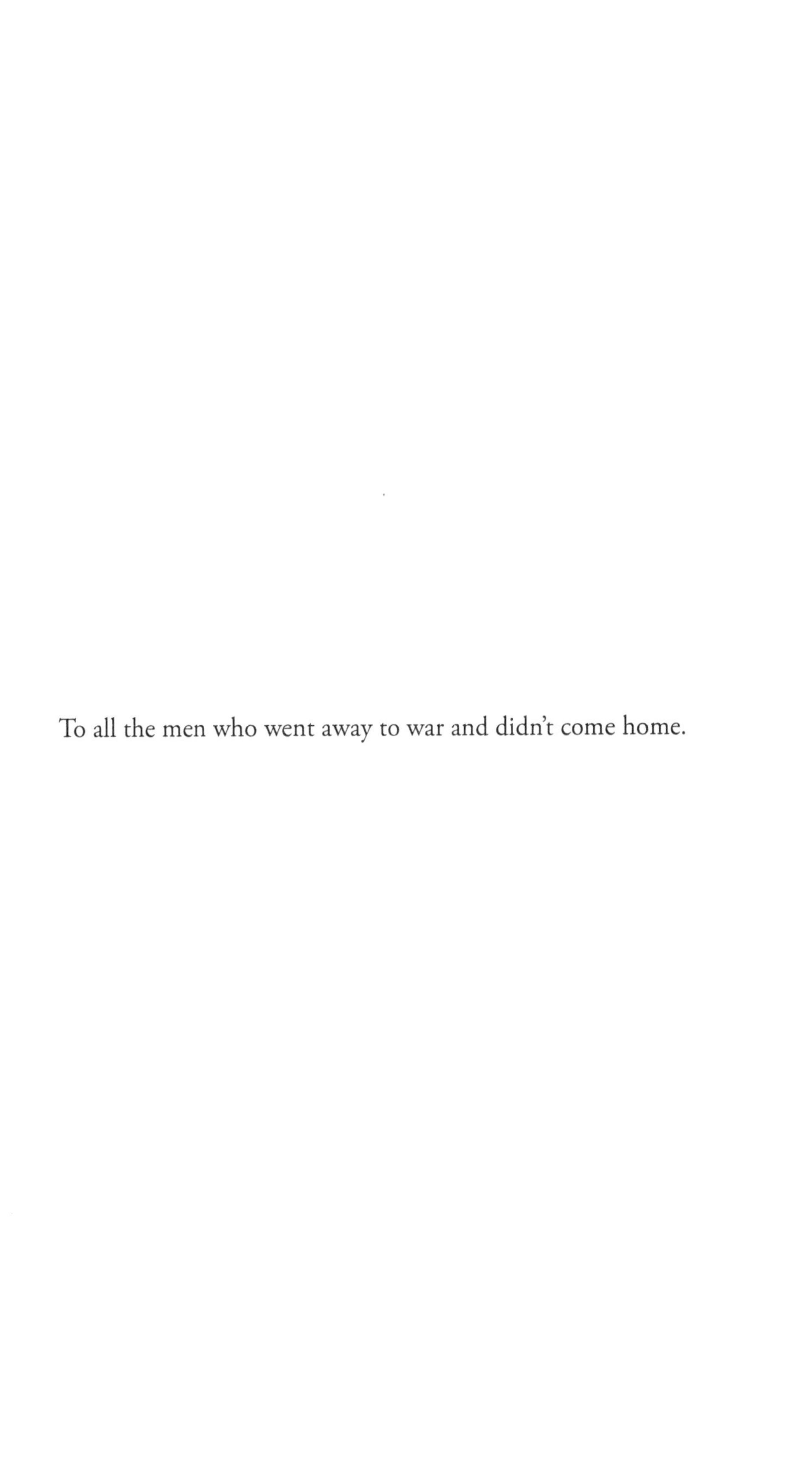

To all the men who went away to war and didn't come home.

PREFACE

This story is true in as many details as the author can remember. The names of the personnel have been changed.

CHAPTER 1

It all started in 1966. The brass in Washington wanted volunteers for a special unit to be sent to Vietnam. Red Powell was the first man to volunteer from his ship. He was twenty years old and full of fight. He believed at the time that America was right in being in Vietnam, and he wanted to be part of that. He had no idea what kind of unit he was volunteering for; he only knew he had to be part of it.

When he received his orders, they said to report to Mare Island on November 1, 1966. He was given two weeks' leave before he was to report.

When the day came for him to leave for his new duty station, he said goodbye to his parents and climbed on the bus which would take him there. It was an eight to ten-hour trip by bus, and it gave him time to think about whether he had made the right decision in volunteering for this unit. By the time he arrived in Vallejo, he decided he had made the right choice. When the bus pulled into the terminal, Red got off and went into the terminal. He walked over to the information counter and asked the man behind the counter the best way to get to the naval base.

Red went out the front door of the terminal and flagged down a cab. He jumped in and told the driver to take him to the main gate of the base. When he arrived at the main gate, he showed the guard his orders and his ID. The guard told him he was going to have to go to the administration building. He also told Red that if he waited a few minutes, the shuttle bus would be back at the gate. Red went over to a bench and sat down to wait for the bus.

About ten minutes passed before the bus arrived. Red got on the bus, and the driver asked him where he was going. Red told him he was looking for the administration building. The driver told him they would be passing the administration building and that he would stop and let him off.

The bus took off down the road and, after several stops later, stopped. The driver told Red this was his stop and to go across the road to the row of buildings on the right; he would reach his destination. He got off the bus and followed the bus drivers' instructions to the letter. He found the administration building and went in.

Red went up to the counter and waited for one of the clerks to come over and help him. Red handed his orders to a short, wiry man in his early twenties and was told to wait for a few minutes. Red thought the man with his orders, looked familiar. He sat there trying to think of where he had seen this man before. Then it hit him; high school. He had known him in high school.

When the man came back to the counter and called him up, Red asked him if he had gone to Van Nuys High School. He said that he had. Red asked if his name was Jeff Burrows.

He said, "That's my name, but how did you know that?"

Red told him he had gone to the same school and graduated in the summer 1964. They talked for a few minutes about their past and found they had known a lot of the same people. Red told Jeff they would have to get together later and talk about school and some of their friends another time.

Red asked Jeff where his barracks were located. Jeff took out a map of the base and showed him where to go. Red thanked Jeff and said goodbye. After a five-minute walk, Red reached his barracks. He went in and picked the first available bunk. He put his seabag away and then laid down for a while. He was tired and fell asleep right away.

Later, after his nap, some of the other men came in, and they were talking about what kind of unit they signed up for. Red tagged along with some of the other men so he could locate other buildings he had need of.

The next morning, the barracks was called to reveille at 5:30 a.m. Red got up, put his uniform on, and went to chow with the rest of the men.

After chow, all personnel were to report to building "B." He followed the men to building "B" and waited outside for further orders.

After a few minutes, more men came to building "B" until the entire area in front of the building had several hundred men waiting.

At precisely 7 a.m., a LTCDR came out the door and someone yelled, "Attention on deck." Everyone snapped to attention. The commander told everyone to be at ease and introduced himself as LTCDR Jack Jensen. He told everyone to form four lines. Two men came out of the building, one carrying a folder. LTCDR Jensen took the folder from the man and opened it; he told the men he was going to assign them to their boats and to line up accordingly.

He started with T-111-1 and then the names of the men attached to that boat. Red didn't have to wait long; he was on T-111-4. Red introduced himself to the other men on the boat. After all the crews were picked, the men got together to find out more about each other. The rest of that day was taken up doing paperwork. There were a few extra pieces of paper to fill out since they were going into a war zone.

The next morning, they rolled out at 6 a.m. for chow and then for orientation. There, they met the commanding officer in charge of their unit. At this time, they were also given a schedule of classes they would have to attend. Before the end of the second day, Red was called before the CO. The CO told Red he was going to send him back to his previous command because he had learned that Red was an only son.

Red told the CO he didn't want to go back and that, according to navy regulations, he could not be forced to return to his old command. The CO had no option but to let him stay. Red left the CO's office and returned to the barracks.

Next day, all the boat crews were called together at the administration building. They were lined up, and one of the clerks asked if anyone wished to return to their previous command. A couple of the men fell out of line and went into the building. The rest of the men were steadfast. After the meeting was over, Red was called into the CO's office again and told he was being taken off his boat and was being assigned to the staff.

Red didn't know whether he was going to like this change or not, but he really didn't have a choice. Red went over to the unit's office and went in. There was a first-class petty officer sitting at a desk doing paperwork but stopped and turned around when Red came in. He asked Red what he was doing there. Red told the petty officer he was told to report there and to wait for the CO. CDR Jensen came in and told Red he wanted to talk to him about what he was going to be doing in the unit.

First, CDR Jensen tried to convince Red to go back to his old unit. Red stuck to his guts; he would not go back. CDR Jensen then told Red, as long as you're going to stay, he was going to be attached to the staff. The CDR dismissed Red and told him to move his seabag and anything else he had and move to where the staff was billeted.

After moving, Red went over to see Jeff. He figured they would go into town and see the sights and have a drink or two. Red didn't know where to go, so Jeff took him to his favorite haunt, the Salono Bar. It was right around the corner from the bus station. There wasn't much going on that evening, so after a couple of beers, they went back to the base.

The next morning, Red got up early and went to chow. After he finished, he went outside and ran into the first-class staff clerk. His name was Allen Jones. Red thought to himself, *Here is a nice sort of fellow*. He was a little heavy set with a crew cut haircut. Allen took Red over to the staff office and introduced him to the other staff members.

Ted was a first-class gunner's mate who had been in Navy for twelve years. The next was John; he was a third-class supply clerk. When Red met Ted and John, he knew he was going to have trouble with John. John was a self-centered, conceded little bastard with a very bad attitude, which Red noticed right off the bat. Ted wasn't much better.

Allen and Red hit it off right away. That afternoon, Allen suggested that he and Red go to the EM club on the base. They could get a beer and play a few games of bingo. Red was agreeable and said he would like that very much. Neither of them won anything, but they had a good time. They turned in early because their training started the very next morning.

CHAPTER 2

The next morning, Red got up, went to chow, and then to the office. He was told he would have to go through the same training as the others even though he was attached to the staff. The training was tough. Every man had to be trained very rigorously in his own rate, but they were cross-trained for every other job on the boat. The training consisted of classes in engines, guns of all calibers, radios, and, last, how to operate the steering of the boat. Later, there were jobs which Red had to perform, which were the most unpleasant things Red could imagine.

The part of the training Red liked best was the weapons, especially the M-79 grenade launcher. He also had to qualify with the M-1 and the M-14. After the classroom instruction, there was the field instruction. This training would take place on San Clemente Island.

On a cold and rainy Saturday morning, late in November 1966, the entire unit loaded into buses and headed to Oakland. The navy, in its infinite wisdom, had chosen a small private airline to transport the unit to San Clemente Island. The name of the airline was Polaris Airline, which no one had ever heard of before. They were a very small airline with only three planes. One was a C-47, and the other two were DC-3s. They used one of the DC-3s for parts for the other two planes.

Red was on the second flight, which happened to be on board the C-47. There were fourteen enlisted and one lieutenant on the flight. Lieutenant George was in charge of the men with Red.

They boarded the plane and got themselves strapped in. The pilot received clearance to take off, and soon, they started to move. So far, everything was going according to plan.

Everything was going really good for about an hour, and then it started. About seventy-five miles north of Bakersfield, the men sitting on the starboard side of the plane noticed one of the windows was starting to break apart. They watched the crack get larger over the next few minutes.

All of a sudden, the window shattered. The stewardess jumped up and ran to the back of the plane. She grabbed a pillow and ran to the window, and stuffed the pillow up against the window. Then she asked one of the men to hold the pillow for a minute while she got something. She ran to the back of the plane again, and this time came back with a two by four. They pushed the two by four up against the window and wedged it between the seats to hold it in place. That solved that problem for the moment.

A little while later, Red was looking out the window and noticed smoke coming from the right engine. Pretty soon, the propeller stopped, and the pilot called back and said they had just lost the engine. At this point, the plane was about twenty-five miles north of Bakersfield. The men were starting to get a bit nervous.

The guy sitting one row in front of Red stopped the stewardess on her way to the back of the plane and asked her how long it was going to take to get to San Clemente Island. Her answer was, "I don't know, we've never made it!"

The pilot radioed the tower for an emergency landing. The tower cleared all other traffic, and the plane landed with no further problems. When they landed at Bakersfield, the men got off the plane and went into the terminal. After a while, the pilot came in and told them the generator in the starboard engine had burned up. They would be stuck there for a few hours.

Red and some of the other guys asked which way the bar was, and they headed for it. Pretty soon, all the men were at the bar, including LT George. Five hours later, Red and the men were pretty well intoxicated. The pilot came into the bar and told everyone they could leave.

Everyone stumbled out to the plane and got on board with a little trouble. They noticed the shattered window had not been fixed.

They just added a few more boards over it. Things were set, and off they went again, up into the air.

The plane started over the mountains south of Bakersfield when all of a sudden, the plane went into a dive. The pilot brought the plane back up level but could not keep it there. The door to the cabin came open, and the men could see the pilot and copilot. Red looked up toward the cockpit and saw the copilot take a piece of string, take off his wrist watch, and tie it to something on the ceiling near the windshield of the plane. The watch hung there for a few minutes before Red figured out what was going on. They had lost the automatic horizon, which is what tells the pilot he is in level flight. It seemed to work, so everyone tried to relax.

They went on for a while until they neared the Burbank Airport. The pilot radioed the tower at Burbank and received word that the fog was so thick that the visibility was down to less than a hundred feet. By now, Red and the rest of the men were terrified. The plane started down through the fog. It went down and down until suddenly, there was the runway. The pilot set the plane down, and everyone gave a big sigh of relief.

The plane taxied over to the terminal and came to an abrupt stop. Everyone pilled out the door as fast as they could. When Red and the others reached the center of the terminal, he asked LT George where they were going to stay for the night. He told them they were on their own, but they had to be back to get on the plane the next morning. Red told LT George they would return by 6 a.m.

Since Red was from the Valley, he called his parents, and they picked him up. When his parents got there to pick Red up, he asked if a few of his buddies could go as well. They told Red they didn't have enough room for them but told them they would get a motel room for them. As they were leaving, the lieutenant told them they had to be back at the airport by 7 a.m. sharp.

That night, Red took the guys out on the town to forget what had happened that day, but the next morning, they had to get back on that plane. The next morning came all too soon. They got up, dressed, went to breakfast, and then grabbed a cab for the airport.

They got there just in time and went straight to the boarding area. The fog was still very bad.

Red turned to Lieutenant George and asked him if they were going to get off the ground that day. He said he didn't know. They waited for another hour and were finally given the go ahead to board the plane. They didn't waste any time boarding the plane or in the take off. The plane went up through the fog until they broke into the sunlight at about three thousand feet.

The pilot came on the intercom and said the flight to San Clemente would take about an hour. Two hours later, the plane was still heading west out to sea. Lieutenant George got up and went forward to the cockpit to find out what was going on. The pilot told the lieutenant he was going to make a slow turn and head back toward the coast. After the turn, he still couldn't see anything. The next step was to go down through the fog to find any landmark they could find.

He started down through the fog. The plane went lower and lower until finally he pulled up about twenty-five feet off the surface of the ocean. He flew the plane at this altitude for about a half an hour.

All of a sudden, just ahead, were some cliffs. He brought the plane up slowly until he just missed hitting the top of the cliff. Everyone was petrified. He guessed right, and just ahead was the end of the runway. The plane touched down with a hard thump and rolled to the other end of the runway. He turned the plane and headed for a small terminal.

After the plane came to a complete stop, everyone got off the plane without saying a word; they couldn't because their hearts were still in their mouths. Very shaky, they walked to the terminal where a truck was waiting for them. They boarded the truck, which took them to the place where they were going to stay for the week. For the rest of that day, Red and three of his friends wandered around, getting to know the place. There wasn't too much to do because this was a small island, and it was a military base to boot.

The next morning, after chow, the CO held a meeting to lay out the week's schedule for the men. At nine that same morning, they were taken to the dock, and they boarded a barge, which would take them to the back side of the island for gunnery practice.

It took about an hour to get to the spot they wanted. When they got to the spot, they dropped two anchors, one at each end of the ship, to keep it from turning. This was the seaward side of the island, and the currents in these waters is quite swift. They placed the gunnery range here to prevent anything from getting between the island and the mainland.

The barge was loaded with all kinds of weapons. There were .50 caliber machine guns, 20mm cannons, 80mm and 60mm mortars and other arms. There were several instructors aboard to teach the proper way to fire the weapon, as well as care and maintenance of the weapons.

First, everyone got a chance to fire the .50 caliber machine gun. There was one special target they had for the men to shoot at. It was a large cave at the edge of the sea. The barge was anchored about three hundred yards off the island. Red ran into a couple of friends he hadn't seen for a while, Sam and Jack. They talked while waiting for their turn at the .50 caliber. When Jack got his turn at the cave, he didn't do very good. Sam wasn't much better. Red watched very carefully, and when it was his turn, he hit the cave almost every time. He had gaged the pitch and roll of the barge, which accounted for his accuracy.

Next came the 20mm cannon. This seemed to be a bit trickier for Red. The gun had a magazine on top and a bag underneath to catch the expended shell cases. It fired at a much slower rate than the .50 caliber machine gun. Sam, Jack, and Red watched for a while until it was their turn.

It took three men to a gun. Sam took the first turn shooting while Jack took care of the magazine. Red took care of the bag under the gun. Then it was Red's turn. Sam loaded a new magazine on the gun, and Jack emptied the bag. Red fired all his rounds; then it was Jack's turn. Sam loaded another magazine onto the gun while Red took care of the bag.

Jack got halfway through the magazine when he had a misfire. Not thinking, he ejected the shell into the bag before Red had a chance to tell him not to. Red quickly opened the bag and all the expended shell cases fell out on the deck along with the misfire round. Red reached down, picked up the misfire, and threw it over the side of the barge. Just as the hot shell hit the water, it exploded. When it did, it sent fragments all over the place. Everyone was looking for a place to hide.

In the process of throwing the shell over the side, Red found he had burned his hands slightly. Red had to sit and watch for the rest of that day and the next because of the burns.

On the third day, Red, Jim, and Sam got up late. They dressed in a hurry and raced down to the dock, but the barge had already left for the gunnery range. The officer in charge of their unit left orders with the officer of the day to put the three men to work doing whatever needed to be done. The officer of the day's name was LT James. LT James assigned the three men to a chief petty officer named Jackson.

Chief Jackson told the three to go get something to eat and then meet him back at that spot in one hour. They went to the mess hall, all wondering what their CO was going to do to them when he got back. After chow, they met Chief Jackson back at the location they had been told to go to.

Chief Jackson asked them if any of them had a military driver's license to which Red said he did. The chief told Red to go over to the motor pool and pick up a five-ton stake truck and come back and pick up the other two men. Red went to the motor pool and told the sergeant in charge what the Chief had said, and the sergeant had Red sign for the truck.

Red went back and picked up Jim and Sam. Chief Jackson had his own ride, a jeep. Chief Jackson told Red to follow him, and off they went. They moved out toward the main gate and checked out with the guard. They made a right turn just outside the gate and headed up into the mountains.

Red drove for the longest time, wondering where they were headed and why they needed such a large truck. Pretty soon, they crested the top of the mountain pass, and they saw hundreds of ammunition bunkers. The road split in three different directions. The chief took the road to the right.

It was a very narrow road, which seemed to get narrower the farther they went. About ten minutes later, they found themselves in front of one of the bunkers, which just happened to be farther away from the other bunkers. This bunker had high explosives inside.

After Red turned the truck around, they got out and went over to the door of the bunker and opened it, and they found out what they were there for. The chief told them they were going to pick up three pallets of 80mm mortar rounds. Red's license didn't cover driving explosives, but the chief said it would be alright.

When Chief Jackson opened the steel door and swung it open, they had to let their eyes get accustomed to the darkness inside the bunker. The chief located the light switch and turned it on. It was a large bunker built into the mountain. They found three pallets close to the door and started moving them.

Three hours later, they had the pallets loaded on the truck. They sat down and rested for a few minutes before starting back. As they looked out over the landscape, it was barren but still, at the same time, beautiful.

They climbed back into the truck, and Red started down the road, very slow. Sam was sitting on the passenger side, looking down the side of the mountain. The road seemed to be narrower going down than going up. Sam was getting very nervous and kept telling Red to get over to his side of the road a little more. Red obliged by putting the wheels on his side of the truck up on the bank of the mountain, making the truck tip to one side a little.

Now, Jack was getting nervous because of how far the truck was tilting. And the fact that the load was not tied down made everyone a little uneasy. He thought they were going to lose the load.

About this time, Jack and Sam told Red to stop the truck, which he did.

"What's wrong with you two? Don't tell me you're afraid?" Red asked.

"Red, Jack and I will have a better chance of living if we walk. We're not too sure what would happen if you lost the load. How much would it change the mountainside?" said Sam.

"We'll walk until we don't have to look over a thousand-foot drop," added Jack.

Red drove the truck very carefully up the road until he reached an area where the road widened out. He stopped the truck and waited for Sam and Jack to catch up to him. They got back in the truck, and Red drove it back down the road.

In the meantime, Chief Jackson was bringing up the rear, laughing all the way. When they arrived back at the main gate, the guard told Red to take the load down to the docks, where it was to be unloaded.

After unloading the truck, they went back to the barracks and waited for the barge to return. When it did get back, their CO called all three of them to the office. He chewed them up one side and down the other for missing the boat. This was an initial part of their training. He also told them they had better not miss the boat again while they were there.

The CO asked them what they had done all day. They replied that they had been moving mortar rounds all day. He dismissed them, and they headed for chow. After chow, Jack and Sam went back to the barracks while Red decided to go to the movie.

The movie turned out to be a comedy, which Red had seen many times, so he decided to take a walk around the base and then back to the barracks.

The next morning, they were up bright and early so they wouldn't be late. That's the way it went for the rest of the week.

CHAPTER 3

First thing Saturday morning, everyone got up early and went to chow. After chow, they went to the barracks, packed their gear, and boarded the truck, taking them to the airfield. When they got to the airfield, they found the same plane waiting for them. Red and a few of the other men asked LT George if they could take a different plane. They were politely told that this plane was it.

The plane pulled over to the loading area, and Red and the others got on board. The plane then pulled out and went to the end of the runway and waited for the tower to give them permission to lift off.

The men noticed that the window and the automatic horizon had been fixed. This made everyone feel a bit better about the flight ahead.

The plane finally started to roll. After a couple of minutes, they were airborne. They were on their way back to their base in Vallejo. The flight was pleasant enough until they neared the bay area, then it started.

The wind picked up, and it was raining like nothing they had ever seen before. About fifty miles south of Oakland is about where it started and the farther north they went, it steadily got worse. The pilot radioed Oakland International Airport for landing instructions and were told all the runways were closed because of extremely high winds and water on the runway. The bay had overflowed onto the runways.

The air traffic controller suggested the pilot call San Francisco Airport and ask them for landing instructions. When the pilot called San Francisco, they told him the same thing Oakland had told him; everything was shut down.

The pilot turned east and headed for Travis Air Force Base. The tower at Travis told the pilot there were ninety mile an hour crosswind. He advised him not to land the plane. The pilot radioed back, saying he thought he could make it.

He was given permission to try and land, but they told him, if you have any doubt at all, don't do it. The pilot brought the plane down over the end of the runway and lowered the plane; so the left wheel was on the ground, but the force of the crosswind would not lower the right side of the plane. His airspeed was too high, and he was getting to the other end of the runway in a big hurry.

He decided to take off before they went too far past the halfway mark. He found he could not lift the plane back in the air. The crosswind was holding the plane down against the ground. He kept going and going, but he couldn't get the plane up. The pilot turned the plane, hoping this maneuver would be enough to get the right side down on the ground.

Meanwhile, at the back of the plane, everyone was yelling, cussing, and praying. Some had their heads covered, so they couldn't see the end coming, and some others were in the back throwing up with the stewardess.

The right wing was coming down but not fast enough. In front of the plane, the pilot saw a very large hanger with both front and back doors open. At this point, he could not stop, so he flew through the hanger, and because the hanger blocked the wind, he was able to lower the right side to the ground. He was still going too fast to stop, so he poured on the coal and managed to take off, just missing a row of trees behind the hanger.

He made one more approach, and when this one almost took off the top of the tower, well, that was that. The controller came over the radio and told him not to take another approach. The controller told the pilot to go back to Oakland and see if the conditions had gotten better. The last thing the controller said was that if we could not land on the runway, then we would have to ditch in the bay. We would be picked up, maybe?

The pilot turned the plane back for Oakland. He radioed Oakland tower and told the controller that if he could not land, he was going to have to ditch in the bay because he was almost out of fuel as well. He didn't have enough gas to go anywhere else.

The tower came back and approved his landing there. The controller also told him there were crosswinds of over eighty miles per hour. The pilot acknowledged that fact and started down.

The wind was blowing so hard that the rain was going parallel to the ground. He brought the plane down until the left wheel was touching the ground through six inches of water. Red was sitting on the left side of the plane next to a window. He could see the wing tip slicing through the water inches above the ground.

The stewardess was still in the restroom with her head in the commode. Meanwhile, the pilot tried to get the right wing down but couldn't. He finally cut both engines and turned the wheel to the right as hard as he could. The plane slowly inched its way down toward the ground. Finally, the right wheel touched down, and a large sigh of relief went up in the back of the plane.

The plane finally came to a stop a few feet away from the end of the terminal. Everyone started for the door on the plane all at the same time. Red, Sam, and Jack were in the middle of the pack and nearly got pushed to the floor and trampled. Meanwhile, the stewardess was still in the John, still sick.

The door opened, and the men piled out, bent down, and kissed the ground through the water. They were very thankful that they had made it. Then they all headed for the bar in the terminal.

Chapter 4

The first week in December 1966, the command was notified that they had to go to SERE training. SERE stands for survival, escape, resistance, and evasion. The course was to be held at Warner Springs, outside of San Diego in the mountains.

First, the whole command was flown to the naval base in San Diego and not on the same airline as before. Then, by bus, to the camp at Warner Springs. Upon arrival, the men went through an orientation class on what was going to happen during the week.

The first four days were spent living off the land. The only thing each man was given was a piece of string and a half of a parachute, nothing else. During those days, the men got to know each other really well as if they were brothers. Red, Sam, and Jack managed to stay together in a group along with six other men.

During the first day, they were taught how to set snares and what kind of wild plants they could eat. They learned that certain barks of trees could be eaten, as well as some roots and berries. After this training, they were left to their own devices.

All day they gathered wild potatoes, onions, and various leafy vegetables. Three of the men snared a couple of rabbits. Some men found a ground squirrel, and others found some grubs. Three rabbits and the other food they had collected didn't go very far, but somehow, they made due.

The first night got very cold, so instead of sleeping separately, they used one parachute half to make a tepee. After the tepee was set up, Sam, Jack, and Red cut some pine branches and laid them inside the tepee. Then they took half of the remaining parachutes and laid them over the branches. The men then crawled on the chutes and pulled all the remaining chutes over themselves. They all got as close to each other as they could to keep warm.

The next morning, Red got up and discovered why it had been so cold that night. There was an inch of fresh snow on the ground. Red woke the others and told them it had snowed that night. They all rolled out of their Mig shift bed, very sore and stiff from sleeping on the branches. They were hungry and started looking for something to eat but didn't find much.

A while later, the officer in charge called everyone together and told the men they were going on a walk that morning. A short walk of only ten or so miles. The hike had two purposes: to find food and to keep their body's fit. The hike took nearly all day, and they didn't find much to eat. They were, on the other hand, very tired.

That night was just as cold as the night before, except they were so tired they didn't mind the cold as much. The next two nights were almost as bad but not quite. On the fourth day, the men in charge of the camp brought twelve rabbits and some vegetables for the total number of men, which was seventy-five. Some of the men cleaned the rabbits to put into a stew. Others looked for more wild vegetables. After everything was ready, they put all the items in a large pot and boiled them for a long time. It took several hours to cook. After eating, some of the men became sick from the mixture, but most were all right. The fourth night wasn't as cold as the previous nights had been.

The fifth morning started the evasion part of the training. The men were loaded onto trucks and taken to the evasion course they were to run. Red, Sam, and Jack were in the last truck, which put them at a distinct disadvantage.

The instructors told the men they had one hour to evade them and to get to a white flag they had set up at the bottom of the course. If they made it to the flag before the hour was up, they would not be harassed. Since Red, Jack, and Sam got there late, they didn't have an hour. They just got started when they had to take cover under a bush. One of the instructors was very close, and they didn't want to be detected.

When they dove under the bush, they were surprised to find another man under the same bush. This man's name was Tom. They all became statues for a moment because of the instructor. He walked over to the bush and called out, "*Get out from under that bush!*"

Red, Sam, and Jack never moved, but Tom got up and went to the instructor. He called out again, only the tone of his voice changed. They still didn't move.

The instructor walked over to the bush and put his foot right in the middle of Sam's back, and told him, "*Stand up, hands over your head.*"

Sam stood up, as did Jack and Red. They put their hands over their heads. The instructor marched them to the truck and had them climb in.

The next phase was the hardest part. The resistance and escape part of the training was set up at a simulated concentration camp. The enclosure was about 150 feet square, thirty feet high, and it was made of barbed wire and concertina wire. At the rear of the enclosure was a forty-foot guard tower with one guard standing next to a .50 caliber machine gun. The gun was loaded with live ammo. On the south side was a hole in the ground that was filled with water. In the middle of the compound were three dugouts used for shelter. The dugouts had rows of bunks inside. At the front of the compound was a small building, which at first, didn't seem to have a purpose.

The trucks pulled up to this small building and stopped. The instructors got out and had the men get out of the trucks. While they were standing there, another set of men came up to them, only this time they were wearing red Chinese uniforms.

Red, Sam, and Jack were in the last truck, so they were the first to go in. They were forced to crawl into an enclosure on their hands and knees. There wasn't enough room to stand because they had run barbed wire across the enclosure about three feet above the ground. Alongside this enclosure was a small building. At the bottom of the building near the ground were five narrow slots where a man could barely squeeze through. At the insistence of the guards, five men at a time went through these slits. About five minutes later, five more men went through. Red had no idea what was going on until it was his turn.

When Red entered, there was a guard standing on a platform above him. The guard told him to remove his clothing and hand it up for inspection. Red did as he was told. After searching his clothing, the guard threw them back down to Red along with a piece of rawhide with a round disk with a number on it. The number stamped on the metal disk was the number ten. The guard told Red to put the rawhide around his neck, hold all his clothes in his arms, and crawl on his knees behind the man on his right.

The five men in the enclosure all marched out on their knees in a single line. As they came out into the main part of the compound, a guard was standing there and instructed them to go over to where the camp commandant was sitting and report to him. The guard also told them to be at attention the whole time they were crawling on their knees.

When Sam got up to the commandant he was asked, "What is your number?"

Sam said, "Sir, my number is eight, sir."

Sam was dismissed and was allowed to go to one of the dugouts still at attention on his knees. Jack was next, and he made it through all right. Next, it was Red's turn. When Red came up in front of the commandant, he must have done something wrong. As soon as Red started to say something, the commandant got off the chair he was sitting on and hit Red across the face with a riding crop. Red fell over with the blow and was then promptly kicked. He didn't say a word; he picked himself up and got back to attention. He was then instructed to go over with the others. The pain he felt was slight compared to the hate he was feeling.

It took several hours for everyone to go through this indignity. At the end of this, a guard came into the compound and announced that six numbers would be called at a time. When these numbers were called, those men were to come to the gate and line up.

Red, Sam, and Jack were in the second group called. They lined up at the gate and were instructed to put their arms under the armpits of the man in front of him and then to put his hands locked behind his head. They were then marched out of the compound as hard as that was.

The guard then marched them through the gate a little way and ordered them to stop. The guard took the three men at the tail end and put them in wooden boxes that were in the ground. Next, he put Red, Sam, and Jack in two by two three-foot boxes above ground. The boxes were built so you were forced to stay in a fetal position. Jack and Sam crawled in on their hands and knees, but Red decided to get in, so he was on his back. This proved to be the best way. Then all six were left in the boxes for one to three hours at a time.

The boxes of the first three men were put in had turn screws on top so they could be tightened down on the man inside. One of the guards would periodically come over and give one of the turn screws down a little tighter. After a while, he got one of the screws so tight, the man started yelling. He kept yelling, and the guard kept tightening the screw. Finally, the man was yelling so loud the guard was told to unscrew the top of the box and find out what the man was yelling about.

When they got the lid off, they discovered the man had a very badly broken arm. He was taken to the hospital. A while later, a guard came back and let the five other men out of the boxes and returned them to the compound. After all the men had gone through being tortured, the next phase would prove to be almost as bad.

The guards came into the compound and pulled the men out in the same order they had done earlier, but this time they were taken to trailers. One man per trailer. The trailers were divided so that two rooms were made from each trailer. Jack was put in one side, and Red was put in the room at the other end of the trailer. In each room was an interrogator.

Red had just stepped into the room when he heard something hit the wall behind him. He looked back to see a short man walking toward him. This was Red's interrogator. He asked Red what his name was.

Red said, "Sir, my name is." That's as far as he got. The interrogator hit him in the mouth, sending him into the corner of the room.

Red tried to get up, but the guy walked over, pulled him up, and hit him again. Red went down again; this time, he saw stars.

The interrogator walked away, leaving Red crumpled up in the corner. Red took his time getting up, and when he did, the guy started asking him questions about his unit, where they were located, his CO's name, and what kind of unit he was with.

Red said, "Sir, under the Geneva Convention, I am only required to give you my name, rank, and serial number, sir." The interrogator was very angry and knocked Red down and kicked him. After this repeated treatment, he was taken back to the compound.

Red got together with Sam and Jack in the compound, and they discussed what they had gone through. After that, they tried to get some sleep, but that didn't come to pass.

The officer in charge was not made to go through the same ordeal as the men. They had other plans for him. Whenever he complained about the treatment of the men, he was made to jump into a hole filled with water and then made to roll around on the ground until told not to.

The next morning, they were released and given a good meal. Most of the men were sick by this time; eating just made them sicker. The trucks that had brought them were waiting to take them back to the base in San Diego for debriefing and a change of clothes. The next morning, they were taken to the airfield and headed back to Vallejo and Mare Island.

CHAPTER 5

Returning to Mare Island after Christmas leave, they resumed their training. The boats they had been waiting for were finally delivered. They were converted landing craft. There were several things added to them, such as four .30 caliber machine guns, two .50 caliber machine guns, and a 20mm cannon. Their training was starting to make sense.

The men now trained on the boats, running up the delta region of the Sacramento River in California. When not on the boats, they were qualifying on the M-1 Garand rifle, the .45 automatic, and the M-79 grenade launcher.

One day in January, twenty of the men were taken to the range to shoot the M-79. Sam and Red were among the twenty. They boarded a truck and were taken to an area of the base that was all marshland. After a short drive, they reached the area.

The instructor was waiting to give the men a short course in the proper way to shoot the weapon. Sam was the first to shoot the M-79 and found it very uncomfortable with the stock sitting in the middle of his chest. According to the instructor this was the proper way to fire the weapon.

The target was an old tank located about 1,500 yards from where they were standing. Sam loaded the shell, put the stock on his chest, sighted it in, and pulled the trigger. The shell fell short of its target by about a hundred feet. Not a bad start for his first time. He tried two more times but did not hit the target. He was able to get a bit closer each time.

Red was next. He had listened to the instructor very close. He took the weapon, loaded it, and took aim. He fiddled around with the sights until he had them just where he wanted them. He finally pulled the trigger and waited.

The shell came down right on top of the turret of the tank. It was a direct hit. The instructor told Red that was an excellent shot and a lucky one for his first time shooting the weapon. Red loaded another shell and fired again. The shell came down in the exact spot as the first one had. The instructor asked Red if he had ever fired an M-79 before, to which he replied that he had never shot one before.

Red loaded his last shell, took aim, and fired. When the shell came down, it hit the same place the other two had hit.

The instructor said, "This is incredible, how did you do that?"

Red said, "Do you see that wire up there in front of us?"

"Yes," he said.

Red continued, "I put the top of the front sight on that wire and pulled the trigger and got lucky."

The instructor shook his head then dismissed Red. After everyone had finished, they got back on the truck and were taken back to the barracks.

The next few days were spent practicing with the M-1 rifle and the .45 auto. At the end of the week, they all had to qualify. On Friday, Red and some others were taken to the range where they were to qualify with the M-1 at a distance of five hundred yards. After qualifying on the M-1, they were moved to another range to qualify on the .45 automatic. During that month, there was more training on different weapons.

Around the end of February 1967, the command made the move to San Diego to await orders. While in San Diego, the following two weeks were spent in classroom studies on enemy recognition, customs, and so on.

On March the 15 and 16, the entire command left San Diego by plane and flew to Travis Air Force Base. At Travis, they topped off the fuel tanks before heading for Hawaii.

They arrived in Hawaii late in the day and stayed for the night. The next morning after chow, they took off again; this time headed for Wake Island, the Alamo of the Pacific.

Wake Island is a very small island about a half-mile wide by about two miles long. The runway is curved and banked because of the size of the island. They arrived about 1 p.m. for refueling and for lunch. The men were met on the runway and taken to the other end of the island for lunch.

When they arrived, they were taken to an old building made of concrete with walls about two feet thick. It was built at the time of WWII. It was also the coolest place on the island. Red and the others thought they were going to die from the extreme heat, especially after they found a thermometer which read 122 degrees. And that was on the shady side of the building.

Here, they were given a boxed lunch and one hour to eat. While eating lunch on Wake, they thought, *How could so much death have happened in such a beautiful place?* Outside of the heat, it was a paradise.

After lunch, they were taken back to the airfield and boarded the plane for another destination. This time it was Okinawa. They arrived on the island at Futenma Air Base about six in the evening. The men were told they could have liberty here, but Red was so tired he decided to stay and get some sleep. Some of the men went on liberty and tried to get Red to go with them, but he declined their invitation.

The next morning, Red dragged himself out of bed, showered, got dressed, and then went to chow. He saw Sam and Jack there and asked them where they had gone. They didn't remember much except it was hot and wet.

After chow, they went to the airfield and boarded the plane. This would be the last leg of their journey. The next stop was Vũng Tàu, South Vietnam.

Landing at Vũng Tàu was like nothing they had ever experienced. As the plane neared the coast, it increased in altitude very rapidly. As the plane reached the runway, the pilot put the plane into a very steep descent.

Red found out later that this type of approach and landing was standard procedure because it was supposed to prevent the planes from getting shot full of holes.

After the plane had landed, they discovered that there were a dozen bullet holes in the side of the plane from small arms fire they had received while landing. This was to be expected; Red found out after a short time later.

CHAPTER 6

Red was finally in Vietnam. After spending nearly three days on a plane, he finally set foot *in-country*, as they called it. The plane taxied over near the navy docks to let the men and their gear out. The plane came to a stop; Red grabbed his seabag and left the plane. He and some of the other men dropped their gear at the dock and wondered over near the water. They hadn't been there more than an hour, when a very loud explosion nearly knocked them down.

About a hundred feet away from where Red and his friends were standing were eight of the army personnel. A young boy walked up to the army personnel and pulled the pin on a hand grenade. The blast killed the boy and seven of the army men. The eighth man had been standing in the middle and didn't have a scratch. Everyone went running to see what had happened and to administer first aid, which might be necessary. For seven of them, it was too late. The little boy was gone; there was nothing left of him.

This was Red's initiation to Vietnam and not a very pleasant one either. About an hour later, a boat pulled up to the dock to take them to their new home. They were taken to the USS *Colleton*. This was one of three ships attached to the command, and they were painted a dark green to match the jungle.

Upon arriving at the ship, the men were taken to their quarters. Red went with the staff personnel, which had their own separate quarters. They were located two decks below the main deck and below the waterline. After finding a locker and putting his gear away, Red went to find the office, which was set up for the staff. The rest of that day was spent setting up the office in preparation for the upcoming operations.

That first night, a few of the men went to the messdecks to watch the evening movie. Red was tired and didn't stay to see the entire movie.

The next morning, Red went up to the office after chow and waited for the CO to come in. When the CO showed up, he laid out what was to be done for that day, and then he left to go to a meeting with the division officers.

Later in the day, the other two ships showed up from an operation they had been running in the Rung Sat Special Zone. These were the USS *Benewah* and the USS *Askari*.

The Rung Sat Special Zone was an area of the Mekong River Delta. The new gunboats had not reached Vietnam, so the squadrons were using old French gunboats, which had been left when the French had been run out of South Vietnam. These boats looked like they had been used in WWII. Some of them were in very bad shape.

Three days later, they were starting their first operation. It was a search and destroy mission about ten miles up one of the many fingers of the Mekong River. The mission lasted three days and was very uneventful. The main purpose of the mission was to stop contraband from going up the river in small boats to the VC. This particular mission produced nothing.

On the next mission, Red got permission to go. He jumped on T-111-4 early in the morning. In the beginning, T-111-4 was the boat Red was assigned to. He was pulled off the boat and attached to staff. The CO did this because Red was an only son. The CO told Red he was going to make sure that he was going to go home alive and not in a bag.

The boats headed up one of the many tributaries of the Mekong to a position where a report said one of their choppers had crashed with the loss of everyone on board. They searched for two days and found nothing but a side panel from the chopper. This find prompted them to look for one more day, but this turned up nothing.

The missions continued, but nothing important happened for a few weeks. A short time later, the crews were given liberty. Red and Jack went into Vũng Tàu to see what the city and the people were like and how they lived. The most important thing for them at the time was finding a place to get something to drink. They walked around for a while, checking out the shops until they found a bar. They went in, sat down, and waited for one of the girls to come over and take their order.

They were well into their third beer when a couple of young girls came over to where they were sitting and sat down next to the guys. They asked them to buy them a drink, and afterward, they would show them a good time. This was a come on to get them to spend all their money.

Red and Jack left the bar and wandered around for a while. It was very hot and humid, so they had to get something cold to drink quite often. They had been gone several hours when they finally made it to the beach. They walked over toward the beach and found several cabanas where they served food and drinks. They picked one of the cabanas and sat down to have another beer. The view from where they were was quite beautiful. You could see the bay and the ships sitting in the bay.

They had been sitting there for some time when Red felt something pulling at him from behind. He turned his head to see what it was but saw nothing. He turned back around and started drinking his beer again when he felt another pull from behind. This time he turned all the way around and finally saw what had been pulling at him.

There behind him was a very young girl, about three or four years old. Her hands were full of flowers, and she motioned for Red to take some. Red got off the stool he was sitting on, and he knelt down beside her. He reached into his pocket and pulled out some change and handed her a few coins. She handed him some flowers, smiled, and then ran away. Red didn't even get a chance to thank her or talk to her.

The next day, Red got a chance to go on liberty again. This time, he went alone. He went back to the same stand that he had been the day before. After sitting there for a while, he felt a pulling from the back and knew this time what it was. The little girl was back.

Red bought some more flowers from her; only this time, he managed to communicate with her. He learned her name was Lin.

Red talked to her for a while and learned she was an orphan. She was living with some friends and had no idea where her parents were. At this point, she ran off again. Red felt very sad for Lin and decided to do something about the situation. He didn't know what, but he was determined to do something. Red tried to find out where she lived but drew a blank.

The next morning, the entire unit moved their base of operations to Đồng Tâm. It took most of that day to move the three ships and all the boats to the new anchorage. They dropped both anchors, fore and aft, so the ships would not turn on their anchors. They remained straight with their bows, headed into the incoming tide. The tide in these waters can and very often change up to twenty feet or more between low tide and high tide.

The next day was spent getting ready for the first operation in this area. Red was still thinking about Lin. He decided that when they got back, he would find her and ask her if she would like to go to America with him. He decided to try and take her back with him when he went home. He noticed the last time he saw her, she looked different but didn't know why he felt that way. Finally, he realized she was not full-blood, but she was half American.

In the meantime, he had a job to do. The next afternoon, Red was given operation plans to deliver to the other units. The army supplied a twelve-foot John boat and one of their personnel to take Red wherever he needed to go. The two of them got in the boat and headed for the base at Đồng Tâm, which was about a thousand yards away. As they reached the entrance to the small harbor, they could see a canal running for as far as one could see. It ran next to the base and was as straight as a needle. The canal was called Route 66; Red learned later.

As they entered the harbor, they noticed two bunkers, one on each side of the entrance. Both of the bunkers had .50 caliber machine guns pointing so they could cover the entrance.

Another fifty yards, and they came to the beach. Red jumped out and pulled the little boat up on the beach. He asked the guy to wait for him. Red walked over to where some of the base personnel were standing and asked where he could find Major Roberts. He was directed to a trailer some fifty feet from where he was standing.

Red walked over and knocked on the door. He was answered with, "Come in." Major Roberts was sitting at a table filing out some papers. He looked up and said, "Come in and sit down, I'll be with you in a minute."

Red said, "Yes, sir."

Major Roberts finished with the paperwork and put it away. He looked over at Red and asked, "What can I do to help you, son?"

Red said, "Sir, I'm here to give you the plans for the operation, which will start tomorrow morning, sir."

Red handed him the plans and a sign-off sheet showing that he had received the copy. After signing, Red thanked the major and left.

Red went back to the boat, and they left to go back to the USS *Colleton*. He finished delivering the operation plans to all the division officers, which took the rest of the day, and then retired for the evening.

The next morning, Red got up, went to chow, and then watched the boats leave for the operation. Each boat carried twelve to eighteen army personnel plus the boat crew. For Red, the next four days, there wasn't much to do but sit around or play cards.

On the third day, the boats ran into an ambush. They took fire from both sides of the river. The lead boat took three hits from B-40 rockets. One rocket went through the front ramp of the boat, one through the engine room, and the third hit the coxswain's compartment, killing Chief Foster instantly. The rocket had hit him in the head.

The boats immediately fired back, taking out the VC that had fired on them. Several other boats were hit with B-40 rockets as well as small arms fire.

After the fight was over, the damaged boats headed back to the repair ship, the USS *Askari*. The rest of the boats picked up the army personnel they had landed the day before and went back to the USS *Colleton*. When they got back, they were debriefed and then let go to clean up and get some hot chow.

CHAPTER 7

Next, the staff moved their headquarters to a barge inside the small harbor of Đồng Tâm. The barge had no propulsion and had to be towed everywhere. The only thing it had was a small office and some living quarters. There were several problems with being on a boat with no way to move under its own power.

Number one was, while under one of the many mortar attacks, it couldn't move. The personnel on board the barge had to run to the nearest slit trench or underground bunker. The mortar attacks happened quite often, sometimes every day, and sometimes every other day. The attacks never came at the same time, it could be during the day, but most of the time, it was in the middle of the night. Red, as well as everyone, was short on sleep as well as their temper.

One morning at about five, Red was abruptly woken up with a bang. There was an explosion just outside the barge. Red threw on his pants and ran outside to see what had happened. When he got to the railing, he saw a large hole in the ground where the latrine had been. No one knew until later just what had happened.

At the time of the explosion, there were three men in the building. Only one man was killed. The other two crawled to safety from under the rubble. They told the story of what they thought happened.

They said they had gotten there first when another man came in, went over to the commode, lifted the seat, and that's when it went up. The man was killed instantly.

Up to this point, no one thought much about the civilians allowed onto the base to work each day. From that day forward, no civilian was allowed to stay on the base at night. They were escorted out every afternoon before the sunset.

That same day as the explosion, one of the men caught one of the civilian workers pacing off the distance between the buildings. He was quickly captured and turned over to the ARVN troops. What they did with him? Red never found out.

That night about eleven, a mortar attack started. The first round hit the water near the hospital. The next round hit the hospital. No one was hurt. Several more rounds came in and damaged a couple of buildings. Two men in one of the barracks were wounded by flying wood splinters. Then it stopped, just as fast as it had started. About two hours later, it started again. This time the mortar attack was followed by the VC trying to get on the base.

Twenty VC had managed to sneak up to the wire and slip through, but that's as far as they got. One of the VC set off a claymore mine at the wire, and then all hell broke loose. Red was at the EM club when the attack started but managed to get to the barge. From there, he watched the fight as it developed. The battle was a short one. The men at the perimeter opened up on the VC, catching them in a crossfire. They also set off a few more claymore mines to make sure. When the smoke cleared, there were twenty bodies. The VC were all carrying AK-47s. They were also carrying several grenades apiece. This was just one of the many harassing actions that the VC carried on.

While Red was at Đồng Tâm, he met and became friends with the base personnel. One of these was Jake. Jake was assigned to the perimeter with two of his friends. One afternoon, Jake was at his post when he saw a young boy walking toward him. As the boy came closer, Jake and his buddies noticed the boy had hand grenades taped to his body. He was also carrying one in his hand.

As the boy got closer, Jake yelled to the boy to stop, using the boy's language. The boy kept walking toward them. Jake yelled to him again and warned him, but he still kept walking toward Jake. Jake then fired a shot near to the boy, but that had no effect.

Finally, when the boy was no more than forty feet from them, Jake pointed his rifle at the boy and shot him. When the bullet hit the boy, his reflexes caused him to pull the pin on the grenade and in the blink of an eye, the boy was gone. All that was left was a hole in the ground. This upset Jake so much that he threw his gun down and started crying. Jake was taken to sick bay and given a very strong sedative to calm him down. It didn't help much.

Red went to see Jake in the hospital, and he told Red he couldn't go back to the front line. He never wanted to touch another gun as long as he lived. Red tried to tell him that he had not only saved himself but the lives of his two friends. This didn't get through to him at that moment. All he could think of was the face of that boy.

A couple of days later, Jake was released from the hospital and went straight to his CO. He told his CO the way he felt and that if ordered, he would not pick up another weapon. His CO understood the situation and had him released and finally sent home.

After a couple more weeks of being mortared every other night, Red's CO decided to move the staff back to the USS *Colleton*. Just before they moved back, Red went up on the top deck of the barge to watch a squadron of F-4s dropping bombs on a VC position. It was close enough for Red to see trees and other things flying through the air every time a bomb hit the ground. He thought to himself, *Boy, I'm glad I'm not under that stuff*.

The day of the move was a day Red was looking forward to. Living on the barge in Đồng Tâm, he never seemed to get enough rest or sleep. The night of the same day of the move, there was another attack on the base. First the mortars, and then the main attack; the attack came from two sides. The tracers were flying everywhere, but not one was hit. Red was watching from the bridge of the USS *Colleton*, which was anchored in the river outside of Đồng Tâm.

When the shooting was over, only two men were slightly injured, and that was from diving into a bunker.

The next day, they moved the entire command up river to a new location. It was near an old French fort. No one knew how old it was, but it was covered with all kinds of creeping ground cover and bushes. It was built with one side of the fort right on the riverbank with high walls and a courtyard in the center. The northern walls had been removed, and a large level area was formed. In this area, the army had brought in two very large self-propelled guns.

The barrels were so big, a man could crawl down inside of the barrels without touching its sides. The shell they used were as big as a VW bus at two thousand pounds or larger. Red's command was brought in to lend support to the guns.

When the operation started the next day, the boats went to a prearranged location and waited. At a given time, the two big guns opened up. For half an hour, they blasted VC positions, some six miles away. When the firing stopped, the boats went in and dropped off the army personnel. They mopped up what was left and then returned to the boats. The boats then returned to the fort and the mother ship. The next day the command moved back to Đồng Tâm.

CHAPTER 8

The next big operation was on June 16, 1967. All the boats were loaded with supplies and men by early afternoon. They left the mother ships and started downriver to a point five hundred yards away. There had been reports of a VC buildup close to the base, and they were dispatched to handle the situation.

Red went up to the flying bridge on the USS *Colleton* to watch. There was a night scope mounted there. Red watched as the boats headed into the bank of the river and lowered their ramps. The army personnel came out of the boats and were just milling around. After they were all out of the boats, they headed inland, all grouped together. All of a sudden, three machine guns opened up on them. They were in a crossfire, and men were dropping left and right.

One of the men with the landing force was a first-class petty officer named Coleman. When the shooting started, he was still at the boat getting his equipment together. He jumped off the boat and hugged the ground. After surveying the situation, he dropped his gear and moved out to help the wounded. He got to the first man and dragged him back to safety. Then he went back for another and then another.

Red was watching all this through the night scope and felt very helpless because there was nothing he could do to help. After what seemed like hours of watching, Coleman got out and brought back the wounded under very heavy fire; Red couldn't take it anymore, so he went back down to the office.

After a half hour, Red had to go back up to the bridge. He looked through the scope again and saw the battle was still going on.

A few minutes later, Red heard a low flying plane coming toward him. It was Puff the Magic Dragon. He passed over the ship on his way to the battle. He passed over the scene and circled around for a pass. He came up along the edge of the river and banked the plane to get a clear shot.

He let go, but instead of hitting the enemy, he strafed the boats. Thankfully, no one on the boats was hit, but there was a lot of movement around the boats at the time.

The next pass was right on target. After the pass, there was no more firing in the direction of the troops. Very carefully, the troops that were left standing moved to the positions held by the enemy. On the way, they pitched a few grenades just to make sure. All they found were enemies dead. At this point, the troops dug in to wait and see if there was going to be a counterattack. Thankfully, it never came.

In the meantime, a squad of men was carrying the dead and wounded back to the boats. The wounded were flown to an evacuation hospital as fast as possible. The dead were stacked up like cordwood, waiting to be moved to another location.

The next morning, Red had to go to the base at Đồng Tâm. Upon his arrival, he was stunned to see a chopper fly to within five or six feet above the ground and push the dead bodies out the side door into an ever-growing pile. Then the chopper left, and another chopper came in and did the same thing.

As the bodies hit the pile as well as the ground, they came apart in various pieces. There were men on the ground picking up body parts and putting them in body bags. Some of the men on the ground made bets to see which body bounced the highest. After all was said and done, there were two hundred dead and only eight survivors.

That night, Red became very ill. He felt very cold and started shaking. After several hours of this, he was taken to sick bay. There were three other men there with the same problem. A couple of hours later, they were on their way to the hospital near Vũng Tàu.

When they landed, there were several nurses waiting to take them into the isolation ward. The ward had room for about forty beds, and most of them were full. This ward was used for patients with malaria and hepatitis. After assigning Red his bed, a nurse came over and took his temperature and some of his blood. She took the blood by pocking a hole in one of Red's fingers. Every fifteen minutes, someone was poking one of Red's fingers. This went on for the length of his eight-day stay.

During the first four days, Red was given nothing but liquids to drink. His temperature was going from ninety-four degrees to 102 degrees in just a matter of a few minutes. At times, he had as many as four to five blankets because he complained of being extremely cold.

On the fifth day, Red started to feel a bit better and was allowed to get out of his bed. They even allowed him to call his parents using the MARS system. The call went from Vũng Tàu to Manila, from Manila to Guam, from Guam to Hawaii, from Hawaii to Bakersfield, and from Bakersfield to a landline to his parents.

At the time, Red didn't realize that where he was, it was day and where his parents were was the middle of the night. And it wasn't even the same day. Red was told he could not tell his parents where he was or why or anything concerning his condition. All he could tell them was he was in a hospital and that he was alright and not to worry. Red could tell they were very concerned, so as soon as he finished his conversation with them, he sat down and wrote them a letter explaining the whole thing.

When the doctor finally came in, Red asked him what was wrong with him. The doctor never got around to telling him what was wrong.

On the ninth day, Red was released to go back to his command. He walked over to the dock area and reported to the officer in charge. He was told the next boat going up the river was the next morning, so he was assigned a bunk for the night. That night he had a relapse and found himself back in the hospital for another two days.

While he was waiting at the dock to get back to his command, he found all the mail which had not been delivered, so Red had all the mail loaded into a Higgins boat, and he took it with him. When he arrived onboard the USS *Colleton*, he reported to his CO. He told the CO he felt fine but was still slightly tired. For the next two days, nothing happened of much consequence.

It was now July, and the next group of operations was scheduled for an area near the Cambodian border. The move started very early one morning, with the boats leading the way. One unit of boats was in front, two other units flanked the large ships, and one unit trailed the ships.

While going up river, Red noticed an area of land where nothing was growing. It was completely barren. This area had been sprayed with Agent Orange.

Upon arriving at their destination, the ships anchored in the middle of the channel while the boats did petrol duty. At this anchorage, all patrols were doubled because of the proximity to the enemy.

Red delivered all the operation plans to all concerned that night and then returned to the ship. The next morning at 0400, the boats left on their search and destroy mission. The area they were to patrol was called Snoopy's Nose because, looking at the map of it, that's what it looked like.

The first few boats pulled up around the tip of the nose and then it happened. "All hell broke loose!" B-40 rockets came in from both sides of the river. One hit the turret on T-111-8, killing the gunner in the turret. Another hit T-111-4 in the area where the coxswain stands, wounding two men and killing a third. Another rocket hit a four-inch piece of armor-plated steel above the mortar pit on one of the monitors. The back blast caught Jack in the face, knocking him to the deck and tearing through the front of his head.

Choppers were dispatched for the wounded. When they arrived, they met with ground fire but managed to get the wounded out and on their way to the hospital at Long Bình.

The next boat to be hit was T-112-6. The coxswain was hit in both legs by a B-40 rocket. He managed to pull himself back up and kept going. Another rocket hit the boat, and then another. The third rocket destroyed the radio, and the coxswain got hit for the second time. The fourth rocket hit on the opposite side of the boat at about the same height as the first. He was hit for the third time. He managed to keep his wits about him and brought his boat out of the battle area to a safe location.

After the boat was at a safe location, he then surveyed the damage and found three of the men on the boat had been wounded, including himself, and the other men were all right. He turned the boat over to Jeff, who was unhurt, and he took the boat to a secure area; the army had set up an LZ (landing zone). The choppers landed and took the dead and wounded to the hospital. A couple of men from one of the other boats transferred to T-112-6 to help bring the boat back to the mother ship. Because of the battle, the operation was cut short, and all the boats returned to base.

CHAPTER 9

The next morning, the command headed back down the river to Vũng Tàu for rest, repair, and relaxation for two weeks. On the way down the river, Red was watching from the port side of the ship. What he was watching was a plane flying low over the jungle, and it looked like he was dropping something. When the ship got closer, Red could smell something that started to burn his lungs. It was orange in color. It covered the entire ship. Red ran to the nearest doorway and ducked inside as fast as he could. It wasn't fast enough; he got a good dose of the stuff. His uniform was covered with it. When his eyes started burning, he ran to the nearest head and flushed his eyes with water.

Red then went to his compartment and changed his uniform because of the uniform was soaked with Agent Orange that used to be green; Red threw his uniform away. He then went back to the unit's office.

Late that day, the ships anchored in Vũng Tàu harbor. The next morning, Red and Sam went on liberty. They hadn't had a beer in a long time. Red had something he had to do first, so he and Sam went over to the beach area to get their beer. Red was hoping to find the little girl he had met when he was there before. He waited for a while and then started looking for her. He could not find her anywhere. He asked some of the vendors, but they were no help either.

After everything he had been through in the past few weeks, he felt very despondent, so he decided to get drunk. And drunk he got. After getting sufficiently drunk, he went to a cathouse for some fun. It was a hot day, but it was even hotter inside the building. He picked one of the girls and went to one of the back rooms. After an hour, he stumbled outside, a little soberer because of sweating so much. He decided to look around the shops for a while and didn't find anything he wanted to buy. Having nothing more to do, he went back to the ship.

When he got back, he was told the CO was going to throw a beer party for the men. It was going to be held at Back Beach the next day.

The next day, everyone left for Back Beach at about 10 a.m. When they arrived, Red saw a beautiful white sandy beach. He had brought his swimming trunks with him, so he changed and went in. The water was warm and refreshing. He felt like he could wash some of the past off his body. After his swim, he went over to where to party was going on and joined in. He relaxed on the sand, drinking his beer, wishing he was somewhere else. Some of the men got together and built a sandcastle.

The CO's plan had worked. Just for a little while everyone could forget where they were and why they were there. For the rest of their stay in Vũng Tàu, there were things to do and a lot of liberty parties. The boats needed to be painted, the engines needed work, as well as the guns.

At the end of their two-week stay, the ships moved up the coast to a place Red couldn't even pronounce. They were going to run several operations from there. These operations were only to back up some large landings along the coast. It lasted three days, and then they were on their way south. This time they bypassed Vũng Tàu and headed back to Đồng Tâm. When they arrived back at Đồng Tâm, they anchored, but not in the same location they had been before. This made it harder for the VC to target the ships.

As soon as the ships were anchored, Red grabbed one of the army personnel, and they were off into Đồng Tâm. Before leaving the ship, Red got the password to get into the harbor at Đồng Tâm. The entrance of the harbor was guarded by two .50 caliber machine guns with crews that were a little jumpy.

It was dark by the time they entered the channel to the base. When they reached the entrance to the harbor, one of the men at his gun position yelled, "Halt, and give the password!"

Red yelled out the password. There was a short pause, and then the voice came back, "That's the wrong password." The next thing Red heard was the bolt of the fifty go home, and he knew he was in trouble. Red stood up in the boat and yelled, "Don't shoot, we're Americans."

The voice came back and asked, "Who won the world series last year?" Red gave him the right answer. There was another question and then another. Red kept giving him the right answers. Finally, the voice told Red to proceed very slowly to where he could be seen. Red did as he was told, and when they got to the bank, there was that voice with an M-16 pointed in Red's direction.

Red and the man with him showed the guard their ID, and then they were let go. Red took care of his business, got the correct password, and the two of them got back in the boat and went back to the ship.

When Red got back on the ship, he went straight to the office, where he told the CO he had been given the wrong password. The CO apologized to Red and told him it would never happen again.

The next day was the beginning of a new operation. There were reports of an enemy buildup in an area near the base. The boats headed out toward the base, and instead of going into the harbor, they headed up the canal Route 66. The boats disappeared up the canal some two miles and then cut off and went up a small river. About a half hour up this river, they ran into the enemy building, a floating bridge across the river. The shooting began, and when it was over, the boats had lost one man and another wounded. The wounded man's name was Ray, who had his left foot blown off. A chopper was dispatched and took him to the hospital at Đồng Tâm.

The next morning, Ray called the office, and Red picked up the phone; it was Ray. Ray told Red what he planned to do. Red told him he didn't think it would work but told Ray to give it a shot.

After talking to Red, Ray called and asked to speak to Commodore Jacobs. Ray got the commodore on the line and asked him if he would come over and present him with his Purple Heart before they shipped him home. The commodore said he would. Ray also asked the commodore to bring "That Hat "with him.

"That Hat" was an admirals hat the commodore had been carrying around for a long time. It had a lot of extra items on it, such as campaign ribbons and the like.

When Commodore Jacobs went to the hospital to see Ray, Ray asked the commodore for the hat. The commodore presented Ray with his Purple Heart and gave him the hat, which surprised everyone in the command. The rumor was that the commodore had been carrying the hat since World War II. The rumor turned out to be true. It took a lot of guts for Ray to ever ask for it, but the commodore was a stand-up guy.

The next day, Red went over to see Ray before they shipped him home. Red was talking to him and asked him what he planned to do when he got home. He said the navy was going to ship him back east to a military hospital to have a new foot fitted for him.

Upon Red's return, plans were already underway for the next operation. The CO had been working on it in his spare time for two weeks. When it was finished and copied, Red ran the copies to all the officers on his list. One of the copies went to all the staff officers, including the commodore. Red grabbed the copies and went up to Officer's Country.

When Red reached the Quarters, he had to wait in the hallway because of a meeting being held right then. As he was standing there, the commanding general came down the hallway. It was four-star General Duncan. As he came near, Red snapped to attention and saluted the general. The general returned the salute and spoke to Red for a moment, then entered the quarters. The general's aid was right behind him, and as the general went into the quarters, his aid stood next to Red in the hallway.

General Duncan and the officers started talking about the upcoming operation. The general wanted to fill in the officers on the roll the air force was going to play in the operation. General Duncan said that there had been a lot of enemy activity in the area of some of the villages. There were seven villages in that area, and the VC were hiding in them as well as using them to hide in. All efforts were made to get the civilians out of the area, but that proved to be impossible. They would just run off into the jungle and hide from the Americans.

The general said they would land the troops on the opposite side of the river across from this one village and dig in. LT Turner asked the general if the village was friendly or enemy-controlled. He said it was a friendly village, but for this operation, it was to be considered under enemy-control, and that they were going to make an example of it. The general said the village had to be destroyed.

Upon hearing this, Red couldn't believe what he had heard. He decided that when he got back to his own ship, he was going to ask permission from his CO to go on this operation. He finished up with the division officers and headed back to the ship. As soon as he got back, he went up to the CO's quarters and asked to go along. At first, the CO said no, but after pleading his case, the CO said it was alright.

Red went to his locker, packed a bag, and went down to the boat he was going to ride on. It just turned out to be his old boat, T-111-4. Red was very pleased. He stowed his gear and laid down for the night. The next morning, they headed upriver until they reached their destination.

When they reached the place, the boats headed into the bank and let off the army personnel opposite the village. The CO came over the radio and told the boats to pull back eight hundred feet from the village. The next thing Red saw was the F-4s coming toward them. The jets banked and came in over the village. When they were in range, they let go with napalm. All three jets dropped their load and then took off. When the napalm went off, it sent a fireball several hundred feet in the air. The heat was so intense that it burned Red's eyebrows off.

Red looked up over the side of the boat toward the village and saw a woman and two children run out of one of the huts. They were completely engulfed in flames. This was a very sickening sight, and Red wondered, *Why?* They weren't there to kill women and children.

After returning from the operation, everyone involved was told not to say a word about what they saw or had done. This was something Red could never forget.

A couple of days later, Red was coming in the office door when Allen told him to leave and come back in a few minutes. Red asked why? Allen told him he was filing a report which was *top secret*. Red told Allen he had a top secret clearance, and it shouldn't be necessary for him to leave. Allen agreed and admitted Red. Red went over and sat down in a chair next to Allen. He looked over to see what Allen was typing and noticed the name of a guy he knew. Red asked Allen what the paper was that he was working on.

Allen told Red it was a transfer to a hospital. Red told Allen he had just seen Jim, and he seemed to be just fine. Red asked what was wrong with Jim. Allen said he had VD.

Red said, "*What?* What kind of VD has he got that he has to be transferred from the unit?"

Allen said, "It's the kind that's fatal."

Red asked Allen to explain what he was talking about, and this is what Allen told him, "We are sending Jim to a small island in the South Pacific to stay there until he dies."

Red asked, "Why?"

Allen said," Because this form of VD is incurable. Jim will be listed as missing in action and presumed dead." Red asked why again.

Allen said, "Earlier in this war, a government agency developed a fatal strain of Syphilis. They infected the population of whores in the northern part of Vietnam, hoping to kill the VC. It was working well until the first Americans came down with it. In fact, the strain was working so well that this agency killed more VC with it than the army did with bullets. The Americans could not be sent back to the states for fear of killing a lot of Americans."

Red asked how many men had been sent to this island. Allen said that there were over six hundred as of that time, maybe more. This was too much for Red to hear, so he left to think about what Allen had told him. Later that day, they talked more about it.

Chapter 10

For the next few weeks, operations were run up to the Đông Hòa area. Most of the operations went well except for one.

The boats started off one morning, early on a five-day operation. They went up the river for about three miles before coming to the side river they were looking for. They turned and headed up toward an area marked on their maps. When they got to the spot marked on their maps, they turned into the bank to let the troops off. One of the boats let down its ramp, and when it touched the riverbank, it landed on a very large mine, sending the ramp back up right into the faces of the troops, which were starting to exit the boat over the ramp. The blast was so great that it sent the troops flying backward into the boat, injuring some of them and springing the ten-thousand-pound ramp. The boat crew had to hand winch the ramp-up.

Jack's boat had already landed and let their complement of troops off. They then pulled off and patrolled the river. Red was on Jack's boat as an observer; all the guns were manned and ready for a fight. About this time, an explosion rocked the boat. The boat was lifted clear out of the water and then settled back in the water very hard. At the same time, one of the .50 caliber turrets was blown straight up in the air with the gun and Juan, who was holding onto the gun.

Red looked up just in time to see the turret and Juan's legs sticking out of the bottom of the turret. Red yelled to Juan, "Let go of the gun!" As loud as he could. Juan didn't hear Red yelling.

Red watched as the turret went up and away from the boat. When it came down, Juan was still holding onto the gun. He never let go of the gun even as they crashed into the river and sank. Red watched and waited for Juan to make an appearance at the surface.

About a minute later, Juan came to the surface. The boat turned around and picked him out of the river. As the boat pulled up to Juan, Red went to the side of the boat and helped him onboard. As Red was pulling Juan onto the boat, some twenty yards away was a loud explosion, which almost scared Red and Juan to death. As Red and Juan got down to the bottom of the boat, Red looked at Juan and asked him what had taken him so long to come to the surface.

When Red felt safe, he noticed he had some blood on his arm. Not thinking anything about it, he wiped his arm off and forgot about it.

While this was going on, bullets were flying in every direction. No one knew who was firing at who. There was firing coming from both sides of the river and explosions everywhere.

The troops could not make it back to the boats, so choppers were called to airlift the troops out. The whole time the choppers were under fire and took several hits. The boats covered the withdrawal of the troops as best as they could, and then they got the hell out as well.

After the operation was over, it was discovered that the worst injury was to Juan. When he went into the river, he went clear to the bottom, which was very silty. Juan had large, concentric red rings on his body and his face. While on the bottom, he came in contact with some kind of parasite. Juan was airlifted to the hospital, where they removed the parasite from his body. They found out that what he had come in contact with was ringworm. About three days later, he returned to the ship.

When Red ran into Juan onboard, he asked him why it took him so long to come to the surface. Juan said, "I was trying to save the gun." Red laughed.

A couple of days later, Juan was working on one of his boat's engines when all of a sudden, he went crazy. It took three of his crewmates to get him out of the engine room. He was trashing around, and it was all they could do to get him out. They called for help. Red and a couple other men came to help. They took Juan to sick bay where the doctor examined him and determined he had gotten a bad case of heat exhaustion.

The doctor immediately covered Juan with ice to bring down his temperature. About fifteen minutes later, Juan started to come around. He finally became coherent enough to ask what had happened. He didn't remember anything of the experience. He stayed in sick bay for a couple of hours, and then the doctor released him. The doctor told Juan to go below and get some rest. He was to do no more that day.

Juan, thinking he was alright, went right back to the boat and started working on the engine again. About an hour later, the same thing happened to him again. They hauled him up to sick bay again, where the doctor asked him why he had gone back to work. Juan's reply was, "The engine has to be fixed before the next operation. They're not going to keep my boat out of action."

With that answer, the doctor restricted Juan to sick bay for the rest of that day and the next day. After a couple of days, Juan was his old self again.

Shortly after Juan's problem, Red found he too had a problem. It wasn't a physical one but more of a dilemma. A couple of Red's friends, John and Jake, came to him with a proposal. Red said he would listen and then give them an answer once he thought it over.

John told Red that he and Jake, and a few other men, were going to take care of a loose end when they all returned to the states. Red asked what the loose end was. Before they told him, they made him promise that once they told him, he could not tell anyone about what they had talked about. Red didn't like the idea but went along with it at the time.

First, they asked Red if he was familiar with a certain actress who was planning a trip to North Vietnam, and he said that he did. Jake said they were tired of people bad-mouthing the men who were fighting and dying in Vietnam. They decided to make an example of this actress. They figured she was a traitor for what she was doing.

Jake and John told Red he didn't have to go along with it but to please listen anyway. The first thing was for them to meet at a place to be named later when they could work out the plans to make an example of this person.

Several of the men wanted to find someone to take care of their problem, and others wanted to do it themselves. It was decided that the seven of them would do the job. Each man was given a specific task to do. They wanted Red to locate this person's home and to draw a map of the best way to enter the property. Red thought to himself, *This is a very wrong thing to do*, but he agreed. He was a little afraid not to go along with them, considering where they were at the time. People have a habit of going missing all the time, and he didn't want to be one of them.

Once they were all home, they were to get together and abduct the person and move her to a secure location in the desert somewhere.

The first thing they were going to do to her was shave all the hair off her entire body. Next, they were going to pass her around for as long as they wanted. At this point, Red closed his ears and his mind to this proposal but said nothing. When Red did get home, he did nothing about their proposal and forgot about it entirely.

CHAPTER 11

A couple of months before Red was due to go home, he started keeping track of the number of days he had left before leaving the country. He started with a calendar and marked off each day as it passed.

There were two operations within this time period. The first was down near the tip of the country. There was no contact with the enemy because he wasn't there. After returning to Đồng Tâm, Red had something very stressful happen to him.

Red was sitting in the office by himself one day when the phone rang. Red picked it up, and a very excited man on the other end told Red to find someone to go upriver and pick up one of their men. The man was wounded, but no one knew how bad. Red said he would take care of it.

Red ran all over, trying to find someone in charge to tell them about the man. After fifteen minutes, he decided to grab one of the army personnel and go pick their man up. They borrowed a twelve-foot John boat and headed toward the battle.

As they got farther up the river, they could hear the shooting. When they rounded a point of land that stuck out toward the center of the river, Red caught sight of the man. They approached very carefully. They ran the boat up on the bank of the river, and Red jumped out. He went over to the man and discovered he knew him. It was Jimmy. Jimmy had stepped on a booby trap with spikes sticking up. When he stepped on this, the spikes went through his boot and his foot.

He was in so much pain, and Red couldn't do anything but get him back to the ship as fast as possible. Red picked him up and carried him and gently put him in the front of the boat, then Red jumped in. As Red was getting into the boat, he felt something but kept going.

When Red left to pick Jimmy up, he left in such a hurry that he didn't even have time to button his shirt. After he sat down in the boat, he noticed his shirt had several holes in it that weren't there before. He took his mind off that and turned to help Jimmy. Red looked at Jimmy's foot and discovered they were not spikes but punji sticks.

Red took Jimmy's knife and tried to get his boot off but couldn't. He even tried to pull them out, but all he did was cut his own hands up. It seemed like forever getting back, but they did. As they approached the pontoon, Red could see his CO standing there with a pissed off look on his face. When they reached the pontoon and got Jimmy off to sick bay, the CO lit into Red with both barrels. He wanted to know what he was doing, going into a battle without a weapon or anything else. Red explained there wasn't time; he couldn't find anyone else to go, so he went.

Their next move was to a village that was built upon a bluff quite away from the river. Red had made friends with one of the army lieutenants by the name of John. He was from the same town in California. They got along good. John used to take Red into the officer's clubs whenever they were near one. Red was always afraid he would get in trouble but never did. Since Red and everyone in his unit didn't wear any insignia, you couldn't tell anyone's rank.

On a particular day, when John and Red were in the village, they came out of a bar and noticed two men carrying weapons and dressed all in black wearing a very strange hat. When they saw Red and John, they very quickly turned and disappeared. Red and John took off after them, but when they went around the corner of a building, Red caught sight of one of the men going underground. They rushed to the spot and found a tunnel.

Red asked John for his sidearm because Red didn't have one. Red very carefully lowered himself into the hole and sat down for a moment until his eyes adjusted to the lowlight. As the fog lifted from his eyes, he saw the two men. They raised their weapons, and Red fired four times, killing the two. Then Red heard someone moving toward him fast. Three more men with guns were coming. Red waited until he could get all three. He only had seconds to act, and he did, killing all three.

John yelled for Red to get out of there as fast as he could, which he did. Red gave John back his weapon. John asked what happened, and Red told him, but Red asked him not to tell his CO, or he will be locked up.

The next operation was almost the same as the previous one. After picking up the troops, the boats were heading back to base when they were ambushed from both sides of the river.

It was a running fight for a half-mile or so. Air support was called so the boats could withdraw. No one was wounded in this foray.

It was now the end of November, and Red was going home soon. He was being transferred to the base in Đồng Tâm. Before he left, he was called to his CO's quarters so he could wish Red luck. When he arrived, the commander bid him, "Enter." They saluted each other, then shook each other's hand. The commander told Red he had recommended Red for several decorations for what Red had done.

Red told the commander he was grateful, but it was not necessary. The commander disagreed and said it was necessary.

The next day, Red left the USS *Colleton* and went into Đồng Tâm. He reported to the personnel officer who assigned Red to one of his subordinates, which in turn gave Red's details from filling sandbags to general clean up around the base.

The day before Red was to leave for Saigon, he and two other men were handed shovels and hoes and told to clean out a ditch near the barracks. The ditch ran across in front of the barracks. At one end of the ditch was a concrete bunker and at the other was the water. Red and the two men were in the ditch when all of a sudden, shooting started. It wasn't uncommon for shooting to be going on, but it was not common to take incoming machine-gun fire in broad daylight.

A VC had set up a machine gun just inside the jungle beyond the cleared outer perimeter. The two men with Red were the first ones to hit the ground. Red was last. After a few minutes, the shooting stopped. They figured it was over, so they stood up and went back to work.

A few minutes later, the shooting started again. This time, Red hit the ground as fast as he could. The two men with him were at the end of the ditch near the bunker, so they ran into the bunker. Red was in a position where he couldn't go in either direction. The bullets were coming closer and closer.

The shooting lasted about five minutes and then stopped. Red stayed right where he was with his face pushed into the dirt. In the meantime, one of the choppers was warming up to go out and see if they could locate the sniper and take him out. Red stayed flat on his face for about ten minutes. He heard some shooting from the base perimeter, and then all shooting stopped. Red figured either the chopper got him, or the men on the perimeter got him.

Red stood up again, and as soon as he did, he came under fire again, only this time, the VC was on target. The bullets were hitting the ground all around Red. As Red was diving to the ground, one of the VC's bullets nicked him on the right ear, and then embedded itself in the dirt embankment behind him. The bullets were so close he figured if he stayed there any longer, he would have no chance at all.

Somehow, Red got to his feet and started running as fast as he could toward the bunker. He made it just in time; a line of bullets was following him right up to the bunker.

While he was running, a chopper, which had taken off, spotted the VC and sent him to meet his ancestors. After a few minutes, the all clear was sounded.

Red went back to the barracks to clean up, and when he entered, he noticed a whole bunch of holes in the walls. He walked over to his bunk and saw that it was full of holes as well as his seabag. On the opposite side of the barracks was a guy sound asleep in his bunk. Red walked over to him to see if he was all right. He bent over and touched his shoulder. When he did this, the guy woke up. Red stepped back in disbelief.

The guy sat up in his bunk and asked Red what he was doing. Red told him he was checking to see if he was still alive.

The guy said, "What are you talking about?"

Red said, "Look around and tell me if you notice anything wrong with the barracks?"

He looked around and said, "What the hell happened?"

Red sat down and told him the story of what had happened. After Red had finished his story, the guy got out of his bunk and checked himself. He didn't have a scratch on him. He checked the blanket he had over him and found two bullet holes in it. For Red, it had been all a bad dream.

Two days before Red was due to go home, he was airlifted to Saigon to wait for the flight home. When he arrived at the airport in Saigon, he was taken to a concrete structure that they called a hotel. It was surrounded by sandbags and machine guns. He reported to the officer in charge. While there, he ran into an old friend he hadn't seen in a while. His name was Joe. Joe talked Red into spending some time seeing the sights around Saigon. Red told Joe to give him a few minutes to put his seabag away, and then they would go. Red met Joe out front, and they flagged down a cab. It was a ten-minute ride to the downtown area, and the ride only cost them thirty-five cents. Joe had the driver stop, and they got out near a place Joe frequently went to.

They went in and sat down at one of the booths. A girl came over and asked them what they wanted to drink. They told her to bring them a couple of beers. While waiting for the beers, they talked about what each of them had been doing for the past six months. Joe had been stationed in Saigon for about a year, and the last time Red had seen Joe was at his last duty station. They spent that afternoon and evening together talking about old times, and both had a good time.

Later that evening, Red said his goodbyes to Joe and started to go back to where he was staying. He went outside and flagged down a cab. Red no more than sat down when the driver took off like a shot. He tried to tell the driver where he wanted to go, but the driver didn't speak any English. Red told him to go in the direction of the airport by giving him hand signals. This didn't work, and the driver wouldn't stop the cab.

They went zipping around the city for several hours in places Red didn't even recognize. By the time Red finally got the driver turned around, it was night.

As they passed through several areas, Red saw people coming out from underground areas near the street. They were all dressed in black and were carrying guns. Red was starting to get very nervous. He reached over the back of the front seat and tapped on the driver's shoulder, and indicated for him to turn left. The driver made the turn and went a couple of blocks, where Red finally recognized where he was at.

He kept giving the driver directions by pointing in the direction he wanted to go. He finally got back to where he was staying. He got the driver to stop, got out, gave the driver some money, and then went into his concrete hotel. He got off the street as fast as he could.

The guard stopped him and asked why he was out so late. He told the guard his story and then went in and reported to the officer in charge. He told the officer what he had seen a short time earlier.

The officer said, "That's normal, they have the place at night, and we have it during the day."

Red went to his bunk and had a very hard time going to sleep. The next thing he knew, it was morning, and someone was telling him he had an hour to pack and get to the airport to catch his plane. He hurried to dress in his whites and get to the field. He arrived just in time to report in. Ten minutes, he was on a TWA jet ready to go home.

A short time later, the plane was in the air, headed for its first stop, Yokota, Japan. When they landed, it was snowing, and the temperature was about zero. Everyone had to leave the plane and go into the terminal while the plane was refueled. Going from the plane to the terminal was just as hazardous as could be imagined. There was so much ice and snow everyone was slipping and falling all over the place. After finally reaching the terminal, half-frozen, they waited for an hour for refueling. They then boarded the plane, and it took off and headed for Travis Air Force Base without any further stops. Red finally felt like he was going home.

CHAPTER 12

Red arrived home in December 1967, a couple of weeks before Christmas. When the plane landed in Burbank, California, his parents were waiting for him. As Red was walking up the stairway, some jerk spit on Red and called him a baby killer. Red started at him, and his father stopped him. Red was going to kill that son of a bitch.

Red wanted nothing to do with or talk about what had happened in Vietnam. Unfortunately, it wasn't to stay that way.

Six months after Red returned, he was sitting at a stool in his favorite bar, The Tender Trap. A guy came in, sat down next to Red, ordered a drink, and started a conversation with Red. His name was Ted, and he appeared to be upset.

Red asked Ted, "Is there something wrong?"

Ted replied, "If you have a little time, I have something to tell you. Have you been to Vietnam?"

Red said, "Yes, I just got back six months ago."

Ted asked, "Have you ever heard of Mei Lei?"

Red said that he had heard but didn't know any of the particulars.

Ted started, "Lieutenant Kelly wasn't at fault for the massacre."

Red asked him how he knew.

"I was with LT Kelly at a meeting with Major Winstone. The major told Kelly he was going on a mission to the isolated village of Mei Lei and that they were to completely destroy everything in the village."

Kelly asked, "Why? This is a friendly village." He knew there was no VC in the village.

The major replied, "It doesn't make any difference, it has to be done."

Kelly refused. Winstone again gave him the order and also gave him two days to think about it.

Two days later, Major Winstone sent for Kelly. Ted drove Kelly to the major's office. They went into the building, and Ted waited outside the office. Ted said he could hear the conservation because the door to the office had been left partially open. The major asked Kelly if he had made up his mind. Kelly said that he had and that the only way he would do it was with a written order.

Winstone said that he would not give him a written order. Kelly asked him why the village was so important? Winstone said that the order had come down from the commander of all forces in Vietnam and not to be questioned.

Winstone said, "I can't give you a written order, but if anything goes wrong, I'll stand up for you at our court-martial."

Kelly agreed to that and asked when they were to go. The major said the mission was to start the next morning.

At five the next morning, the men started on their way. Each man knew what he was supposed to do.

At this point in their conversation, Ted started to cry. Red asked him what he was crying about.

He said, "Everything you will hear from now on is the most tragic thing you will ever want to hear." He went on, "When we arrived at the edge of the village, the men spread out and started their sweep of the village. We started with the animals and gradually worked our way up to killing everything in the village. We set fire to the huts to drive the villagers out into the open. The killing was horrible, old men and women mostly."

Red could not believe what he was listening to, but somehow, he knew it was the truth.

Ted started again, "While we were killing the village of Mei Lei, Major Winstone was having his own problems. A government agent found out what kind of deal the major made with Kelly, and they managed to get rid of the major. The cause of death on the certificate was a heart attack, but that was a lie."

Red later found out there is a chemical that can mimic a heart attack. The chemical leaves no trace in the body. This was later confirmed by a retired rear admiral from military intelligence. The admiral happened to be one of Red's neighbors.

When Kelly returned from the mission, he found out about the major and became very worried. He thought to himself, *If the press caught wind of this, he would be crucified.* As it is now known, this actually happened. Ted said the military tried to cover it up, but that didn't work either. Kelly had no one to back up his story, so he was put on trial and convicted.

At this point in his story, Ted stopped and said he could not go on. He said he was going to end his life because of what he had seen and what he had done. Red thought he was making a very bad joke and asked Ted why he didn't go to the press with his story. He said that he had, but that they didn't believe him. Ted said the American people weren't ready to hear the truth.

Three days later, Red was watching the six o'clock news on TV when he heard the news that Ted had done what he said he was going to do. Now he, too, was dead, and Red was the only one who knew the truth. Now maybe everyone will know the truth about the men who didn't come home.

Does the story end here, or are there others with similar stories of the truth? I hope this story will prompt others to write their account of what happened *over there.*

God, forgive everyone.

ABOUT THE AUTHOR

The author was from California, now living in Yamhill, Oregon. He is a Vietnam veteran. The story is about River Assault Squadron 11 from 1966 through 1967. The good and the bad.